HOOT'nANNIE

Written and Illustrated
by
Linda Marchus

For My Honey, Val

Annie, the owl, loved to hoot. She hooted at rabbits, squirrels, and snakes. She hooted at fish, frogs, and salamanders. She hooted at cars and she hooted at trains. Every so often Annie hooted at the wrong time and that got her into trouble.

One morning Annie woke up before sunrise.

"Hoot hoot," she said.

Annie's hooting woke up her friend, Owen.

"I'm excited," Annie told him. "I finally have all of my
flight feathers. I'm going on my first hunt today.
I'm going to be a good hunter."

"That's nice," said Owen. He stretched and he yawned.

While Annie was waiting for the rest of the owls to wake up, a car zoomed by. Vroom, vroom, went the car, vroom, vroom. "Hoot, hoot," Annie hooted. "Hoot, hoot."

A train chugged by. Toot, toot, went the train, toot, toot.

"Hoot, hoot," Annie hooted. "Hoot, hoot."

She waved her wings at the engineer.

Soon everyone was awake.

"It's time to go hunting," announced Jasper, the owl leader.

Annie, Owen, and the other owls flew with Jasper to the meadow. When they arrived, they started hunting for breakfast.

Annie saw some rabbits. "Hoot, hoot," she called out.

The rabbits ran back to their burrow.

"Stop hooting, Annie," said Jasper.

"Hunting is a quiet time, not a hooting time."

Owen flew up to Annie. "You're a Hoot'n Annie,"

he whispered with a smile.

Annie saw some squirrels. "Hoot, hoot," she said. Then she swooped through the sky. The squirrels scampered to their nest. "I said, no hooting," Jasper hissed.

Owen giggled. "Hoot'n Annie, Hoot'n Annie," he said.

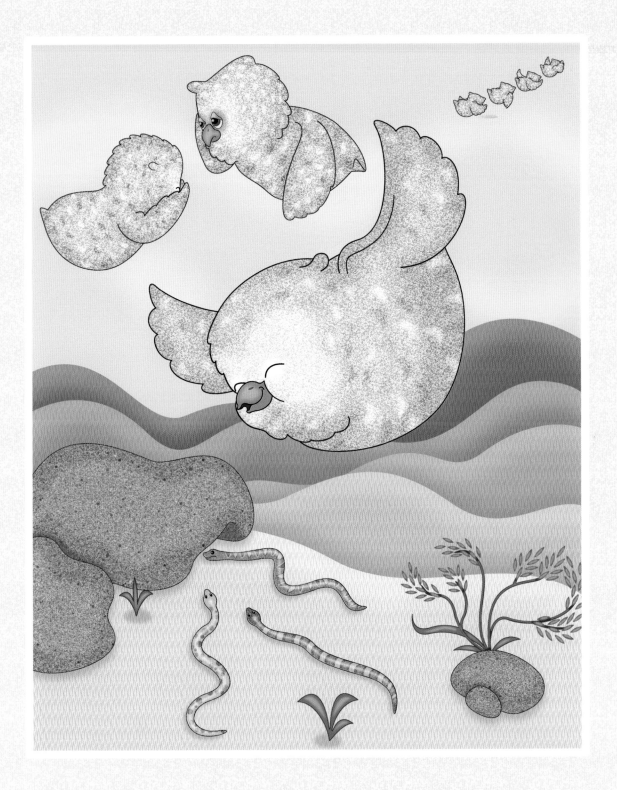

Annie saw some snakes. She zigzagged back and forth, then
hooted one more time. The snakes slithered under their rock.
The owls returned home without breakfast.

That afternoon Jasper flew over to Annie's nest.

"It's time for lunch," he said. "Everyone's hungry.

This is your last chance. If you hoot and scare our lunch away,

I won't allow you to go hunting tonight."

"I'll try to stay quiet," said Annie.

On the hunt Annie saw a fish and kept quiet.

She saw a frog and kept quiet.

Then she saw a salamander scurry across the grass and dive
into the creek. "Hoot, hoot, hoot, hoot," Annie burst out.
There was no lunch.

When they returned to their homes, Jasper told Annie,
"There's a time to hoot and a time to be quiet. You need to
learn the difference. Tonight you'll stay home."

Annie felt bad. "Everyone's hungry, and it's all my fault," she told Owen. "I'm going to practice being quiet for the rest of the day. Then I'll be a good hunter."

That afternoon the rabbits and squirrels played in the meadow.

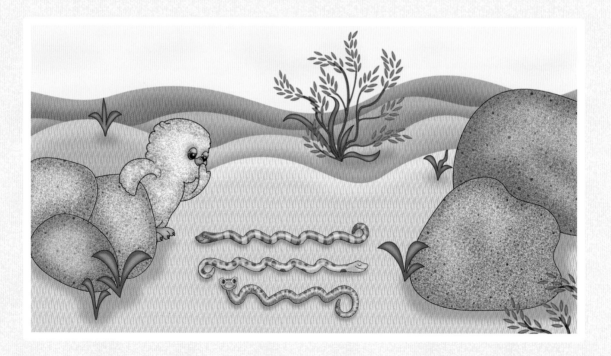

The snakes took a nap in the sunshine.

Annie kept quiet.

The fish and the frog splashed in the creek.

The salamander peeked out from under his log.

Annie opened her beak, but she kept quiet.

Even when a car zoomed down
the road, she kept quiet.
Annie opened her beak and took a
big breath, but she kept quiet.

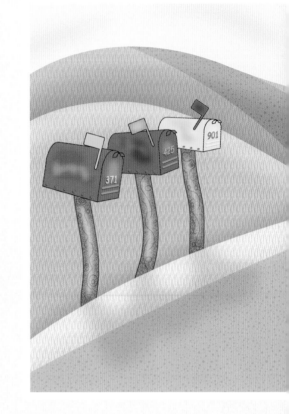

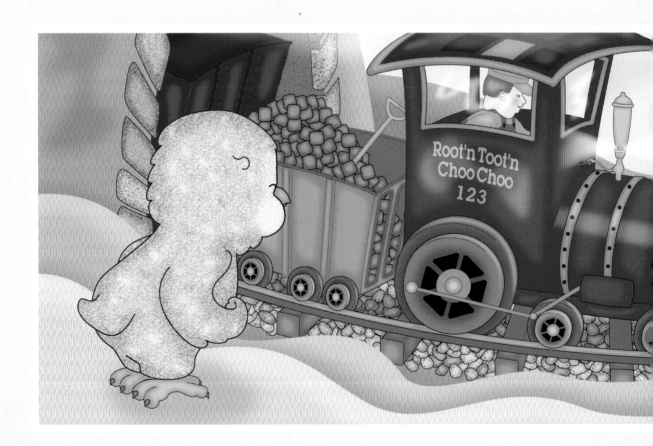

Then a train chugged by.
Toot, toot, went the train.
Annie opened her beak.
Toot, toot, went the train again.
She took a big breath.
Toot, toot, went the train
one last time.
She puffed up her cheeks
with hooting air.
Annie kept quiet.
I might explode, she thought.

When the owls went hunting for dinner, Annie stayed home and watched the babies. It was peaceful, for awhile. Then Annie heard a sound. "Who's there?" she asked.

A twig snapped near the nest of baby owls.

Annie saw something move. It was a bear. It snorted.

Annie's heart was pounding hard, but she didn't hoot.
"Go away," she whispered.

The bear moved closer
to the babies.
"SCRAM,"
Annie said, a bit louder.
Still, she didn't hoot.
The bear growled and
started to climb the tree.
Annie paced back and forth.
He's heading for the babies,
she thought.
I have to do something now.

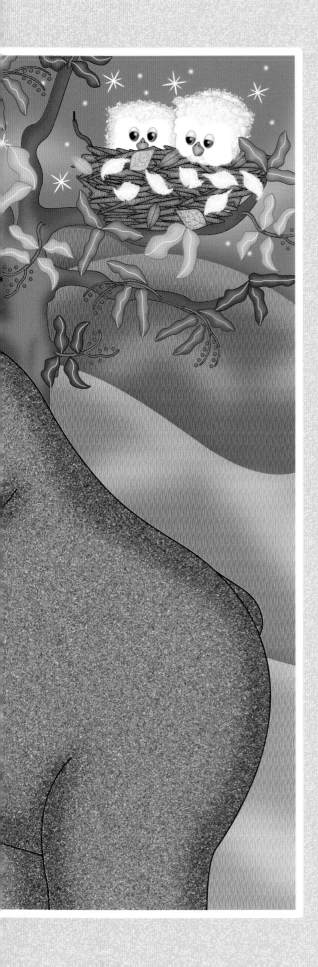

"This is a hooting time,"
Annie said.
She opened her beak,
took a big breath, and
puffed up her cheeks
with hooting air.

"HOOT, HOOT,"

she hooted, at the top of her
lungs. She flapped her wings
with a mighty force and flew
circles around the bear.

"HOOT, HOOT, HOOT, HOOT!"

The bear ran away, passing
Jasper and the other owls as
they returned from their hunt.

"Annie saved the babies," Jasper declared, clapping his wings. "Hurray for Annie!"

"Hurray for Hoot'n Annie!" said Owen. The owls cheered.

Annie hooted.

The next day Annie hooted at rabbits, squirrels, and snakes.

She hooted at fish, frogs, and salamanders.

She hooted at cars and she hooted at trains.

Annie became a good hunter. When hunting,
she quietly swept through the air and circled the meadow.
Sometimes she whispered, "Hoot, hoot."

Library of Congress Control Number:2002110786

ISBN 0-9723122-0-X

Printed in Hong Kong

WEE READ PUBLISHING

weereadpublishing.com